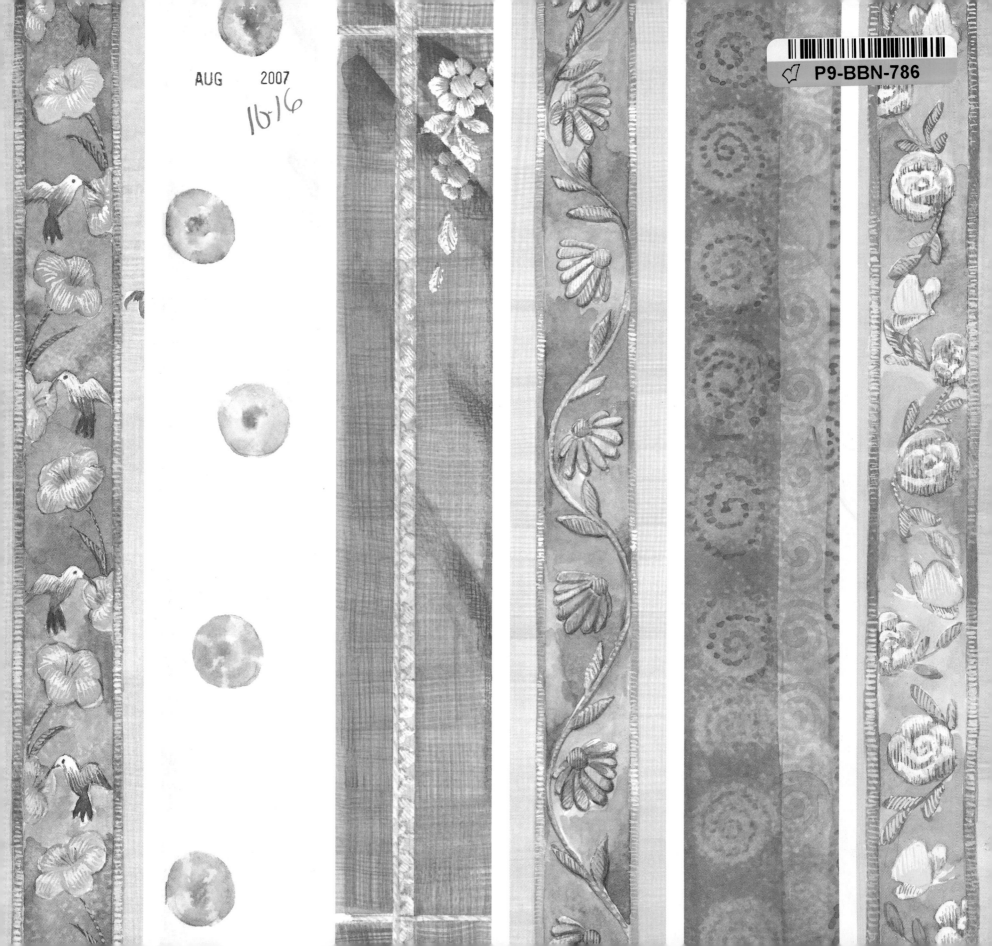

Every day my dadima wears saris—
saris as bright and cheerful as a
bouquet of wildflowers.

WITHDRAWN

She wears them
in the morning.

She wears them
in the evening.

She wears them around the house.

She wears them
around the town.

She wears them made out of cotton.

She wears them made out of silk.

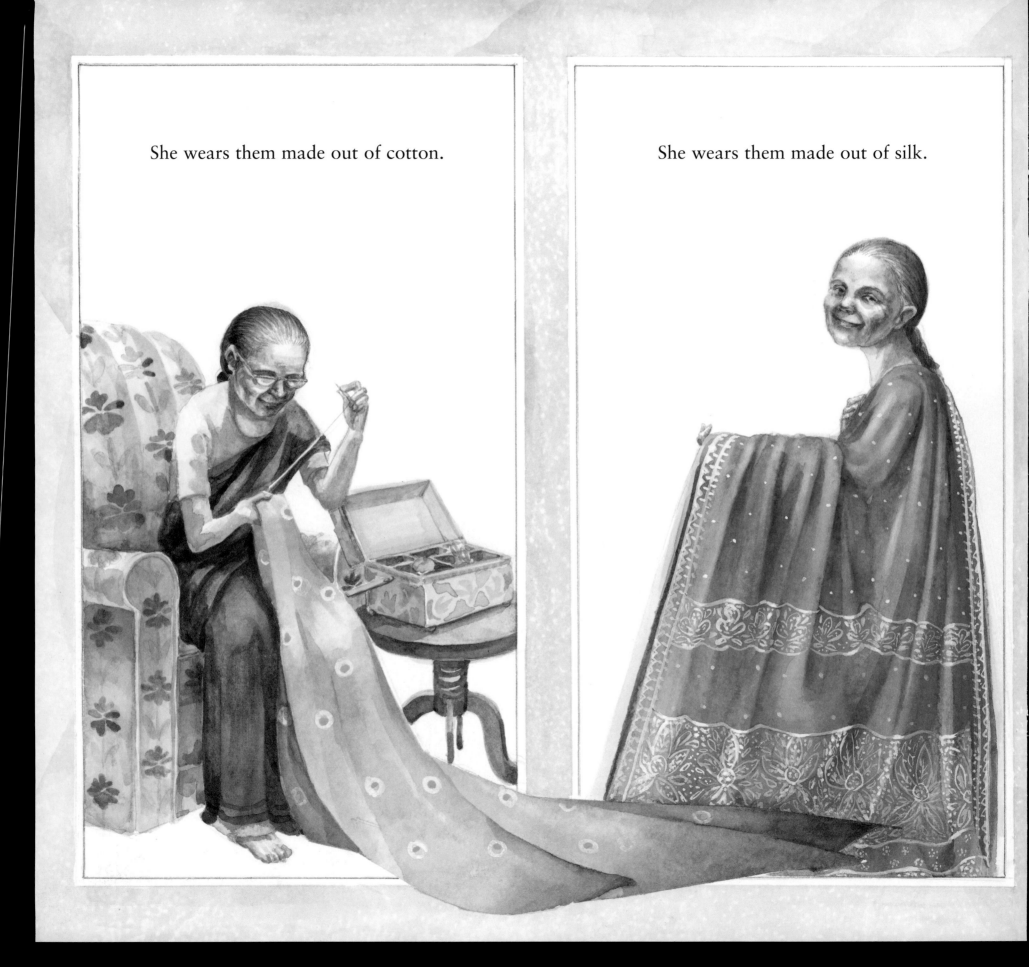

Sometimes she tucks the *pallu*,
the end of her sari, tightly.

And sometimes she lets it dance in the breeze.

"Your saris are beautiful, Dadima," I say one day.
"But don't you get tired of wearing them?"

"Never, Rupa," Dadima says.

"Don't you ever want to wear a gray skirt and a red blouse
with round buttons like Mommy does?" I ask. "Or a green
dress like me?"

"I never do," Dadima says.

"What about pants with pockets and a shirt with a scarf
around your neck? Don't you ever feel like wearing
them?" I say.

"Honestly," Dadima answers, "I never thought
about it."

"Why not?" I want to know.

"Because a sari is a sari and I can
do so much with it," she says.

"What can you do with a sari?" I ask.

"Suppose you and I are sitting out on the porch and it gets hot," Dadima says. "Then we can keep cool." She begins to fan the two of us with the end of her sari.

"Oh," I say. "That's nice."

"If we go to the beach and collect seashells, we can wrap the shells in my sari," Dadima says.

"Like this?" I ask. I make a pouch with the end of her sari.

"Yes," Dadima answers.

"What else?" I ask.

"Suppose we go for a walk and it begins to sprinkle,"
Dadima says. "I can make an umbrella." And right then
she covers both our heads with her sari.
I like the feel of it, light and cool as a breeze.

"I know what else we can do with your sari, Dadima," I tell her.

"What else?" she asks.

"Remember the Gir Jungle you told me about? The one you went to when you were a little girl? With all the lions, leopards, and snakes?"

"Of course I do," Dadima says.

"Imagine we are in the Gir Jungle," I say.

She closes her eyes and puts her hands over them.

"I see the deep, dark jungle," she says.

"When we go in the jungle you have to make sure to wear your leopard print sari," I say. "Then you can wrap me up in it, too, so no animal will attack us."

"I'll wrap you up," Dadima promises.

"And then if we are caught in a storm and all we can find is some muddy water, we can strain it through your *pallu*," I go on. "Then we will have clean water to drink."

"I suppose so," Dadima says, wrinkling her nose. She doesn't like that idea very much.

"If I slip and scrape my knee in the jungle you can tear away a piece from your sari and tie a bandage on me," I say.

"I sure can," Dadima says.

"And if you forget to hug me, Dadima, I can tie a knot in your sari to remind you," I say.

Just then my little sister Neha comes to find me. "Rupa, Rupa, where are you?" she calls.

I decide to play a game with Neha. Quickly, I cover myself with Dadima's sari. While I am hiding under there, I make a secret knot in the corner of her *pallu*. That way Dadima will remember to give me a hug.

"I found you, Rupa!" Neha says. "My turn to hide."

I come out and Neha hides under the *pallu*.

"Dadima, did your dadima wear a sari too?" I ask.

"Yes," Dadima answers. "And so did my dadima's dadima."

Neha pokes her head out. "When I grow up, will you make me a sari?" she asks.

"You and Rupa can wear my saris," Dadima says.

"But they won't fit," Neha says. She looks sad.

"A sari can fit anyone," Dadima tells her. "Come with me."

We all go to Dadima's room.

Dadima takes out a bright yellow sari from her closet. "Unfold this," she says.

Neha and I unfold and unfold and unfold some more.

"But this is just a lot of cloth," I say, shaking my head.

"That's right," Dadima says. "A sari is a long piece of material that you wrap around yourself in a special way."

"Can you show us more saris?" I ask.

"More saris, more saris!" Neha squeals.

Dadima takes out many saris.

Some are soft and some are stiff.

Some are bright and some are light.

Some are fancy and some are plain.

"Which one is your favorite, Dadima?" I ask.

"I like all of them," Dadima says.

"But I have three special saris."

Dadima takes out a pale yellow sari with rainbow-colored polka dots. "This one is a half-sari. It is special because it was my first sari," she tells us.

Next she picks up a pink sari as soft as Neha's cheeks. "I wore this sari on the plane when I came from India to America," she says.

Then Dadima shows Neha and me a sari that
shimmers. It is red with a *pallu* stitched in gold.
"This is my wedding sari," she whispers.
"It is so beautiful!" I say.
"It is indeed," Dadima agrees.

"Can you show us how to wrap a sari?" I ask.

"I want sari, I want sari," Neha says, tugging at Dadima's *pallu*.

Dadima puts the sari with polka dots on Neha and the soft pink one on me.

"My two favorite saris for my two granddaughters,"
Dadima says. Her smile fills her face like the big, round
moon fills the sky.

Dressed in our saris, all three of us stand in front
of the mirror.

Dadima draws her sari over her head, making a snug
frame around her face. Neha and I do the same. Our
eyes twinkle in the mirror like the golden threads in
Dadima's wedding *pallu*.

"We look like you, Dadima," I say.

"Yes," she says, taking Neha and me in her arms.
"Very much so."

I hug Dadima back.

Then I untie the secret knot I made in her sari.

Author's Note

When I was young I believed that every girl wore a sari when she grew up. All the women I knew—my mother, aunts, and grandmothers—wore saris. Outside our home, the streets were filled with women in flowing silk and soft cotton, forming a moving carnival of colors and patterns. It was not until I saw women in the city of Mumbai wearing dresses that I realized that not all women wore saris.

I wore a long skirt, blouse, and half-sari at my aunt's wedding when I was four. There were tiny gold bells embroidered all over it. My first experience with a six-yard sari was when I attended another wedding at age fifteen. All evening I was nervous, and I kept tugging at the *pallu*. When my older cousin saw that my *pallu* was sweeping the floor, she warned me that if I didn't stop, my whole sari would come undone! She took me aside and tucked my sari back into my petticoat. I was very relieved when I was finally able to change back into a dress.

Eventually, I did grow more comfortable wearing a sari. As a wedding gift, my grandmother gave me a sari that had originally been a turban. The king of the state of Bhavnagar, in western India, had given it to my great-grandfather. The material is bright red organza with gold checks. I cherish that sari as well as the ones that belonged to my grandmother and mother. They are part of my family's heritage. Each sari that passes from one generation to another tells stories and holds memories in its folds.

Today my two grown daughters—Rupa and Neha—and I love to wear saris on special occasions. Rupa is modeling the sari on the next page.

—K. S.

How to Wrap a Sari

You'll need—

- ❦ A lightweight piece of fabric 6 yards long, or a ready-made sari

- ❦ A matching blouse, or *choli*

- ❦ A waist-to-ankle drawstring petticoat

Put on the blouse and pull the drawstring of your petticoat tightly at the waist.

Unfold the sari and grasp the plain end of the fabric, keeping most of the material to your left.

Starting from a point to the right of your navel, tuck the top edge of the sari's plain end into the petticoat, making one complete turn of the material around your waistline. Be sure that the sari's hem touches the floor.

Beginning from the tucked-in end, make pleats about 5 inches wide in the sari. Create 8 to 10 even pleats and hold them up together, making sure that they fall straight. Now turn the pleats so they open toward your left. You can use a safety pin to hold the pleats together before tucking them into the waistband, slightly to the left of your navel.

Wrap the sari around yourself once more, without tucking it in the petticoat. Holding the top edge of the sari, bring the remaining fabric up under your right arm and drape it over your left shoulder.

The end of the sari should fall to your knees or slightly below. The end portion from the left shoulder down is called the *pallu*. If you'd like, you can pin the *pallu* at the shoulder to prevent it from slipping off.